Hello, you!

Oh, please don't look
inside the pages
of this book.

Turn around and quickly run ...

The
SCHOOL
of
MONSTERS
has begun!

SCHOOL OF MONSTERS

By Sally Rippin

BAT-BOY TIM SAYS BOO!

Art by Chris Kennett

Kane Miller
A DIVISION OF EDC PUBLISHING

Some are scaly,
some have hair.

Some monsters vanish into air!

PUFF!

Like Bat-Boy Tim
who loves to play

by always getting
in the **way**.

PA-DOOF!

Tim can change from boy to **bat**

POW!

so no one knows
where Tim is **at**.

Just when Sam
has left the room,

Tim appears and shouts out, "Boom!"

William looks from side to **side**

to see where Bat-Boy
Tim might hide.

BOO!

POOT!

Mary tries to
read her book.

But Tim is there to take a look.

HA!

"Stop it, Tim!" the
monsters say.

"You creep us out!
Just go **away**!"

Poor old Tim just wants to play,

but scaring friends
is not the **way**.

How can Tim still have his **fun**?

Now when he flies, the others run!

SWOOP!

But having wings is useful, too

and Bat-Boy Tim knows
what to do.

At lunchtime when
the class is out ...

Bat-Boy Tim flies all about.

A paper here,
a paper there,

SWISH!

on books and tables,
on a chair.

SWOOSH!

One by one they find a note

and show each other
what Tim **wrote**.

Tim changes then from bat to kid.

BLOOF!

They're happy now.
See what he **did**?

It's cool to hang down
from the **wall**,

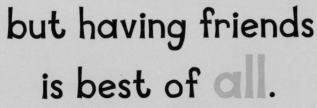

but having friends
is best of all.

look

say

chair

run

play

room

do

too

away

did

note

there

boo

way

all

side

wrote

out

wall

about

HOW TO USE THIS BOOK

for adults reading with children

Welcome to the School of Monsters!

Here are some tips for helping your child learn to read.

At first, your child will be happy just to listen to you read aloud. Reading to your child is a great way for them to associate books with enjoyment and love, as well as to become familiar with language. Talk to them about what is going on in the pictures and ask them questions about what they see. As you read aloud, follow the words with your finger from left to right.

Once your child has started to receive some basic reading instruction, you might like to point out the words in **bold**. Some of these will already be familiar from school. You can assist your child to decode the ones they don't know by sounding out the letters.

As your child's confidence increases, you might like to pause at each word in bold and let your child try to sound it out for themselves. They can then practice the words again using the list at the back of the book.

After some time, your child may feel ready to tackle the whole story themselves. Maybe they can make up their own monster stories, too!

Sally Rippin is one of Australia's best-selling and most-beloved children's authors. She has written over 50 books for children and young adults, and her mantel holds numerous awards for her writing. Best known for her *Billie B. Brown*, *Hey Jack!* and *Polly and Buster* series, Sally loves to write stories with heart, as well as characters that resonate with children, parents, and teachers alike.

HOW TO DRAW BAT-BOY TIM

① Using a pencil, start with 2 circles for eyes, a pointy nose, and a big smiley mouth.

② Draw a V shape for the hair, an open mouth, and a bow tie beneath that.

③ Draw a box shape for the head and a rectangle body.

④ Add 3 mountains for the hair, some pointy ears, shorts, and sleeves.

5 Add arms, legs, hands, and feet.

6 Time for the final details! Add ear lines, tongue, and shirt buttons. Don't forget his CAPE!

Chris Kennett has been drawing ever since he could hold a pencil (or so his mom says). But professionally, Chris has been creating quirky characters for just over 20 years. He's best known for drawing weird and wonderful creatures from the *Star Wars* universe, but he also loves drawing cute and cuddly monsters – and he hopes you do too!

WELCOME
TO THE
SCHOOL OF MONSTERS

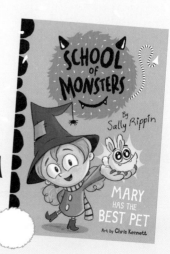

You shouldn't bring a pet to **school**.
But Mary's pet is super **cool**!

Have you read **ALL** the School of Monsters stories?

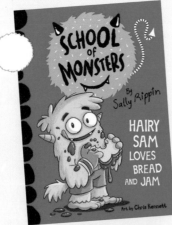

Sam makes a mess
when he eats **jam**.
Can he fix it?
Yes, he **can**!

Today it's Sports Day
in the **sun**.
But do you think that
Pete can **run**?

Jamie Lee sure likes to **eat**! Today she has a special **treat** ...

When Bat-Boy Tim comes out to **play**, why do others run **away**?

Some monsters are short, and others are **tall**, but Frank is quite clearly the tallest of **all**!

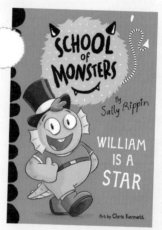

When Will gets nervous, he lets out a **stink**. But what will all his classmates **think**?

All that Jess touches gets gooey and **sticky**. How can she solve a problem so **tricky**?

No one likes to be left **out**. This makes Luna scream and **shout**!

Now that you've learned to read along with Sally Rippin's School of Monsters, meet her other friends!

Hey Jack!

Billie B. Brown

Down-to-earth, real-life stories for real-life kids!